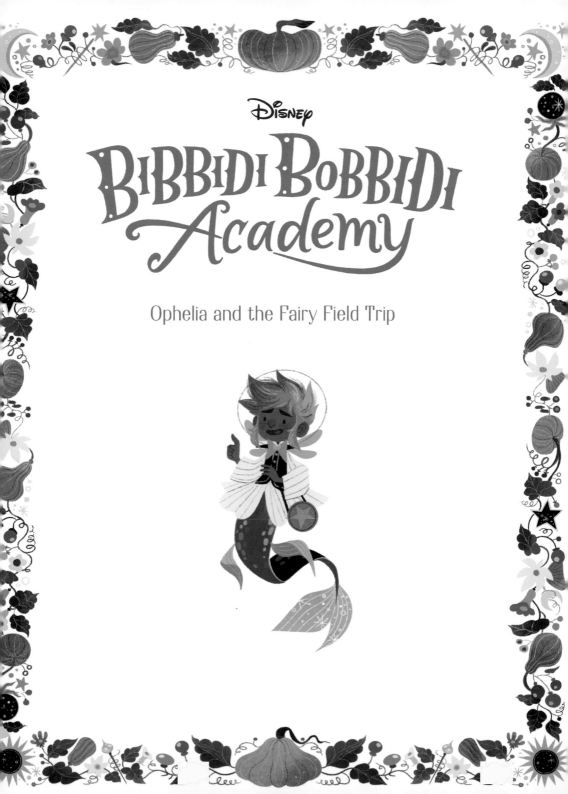

Disney

Bibbidi Bobbidi Academy

Ophelia and the Fairy Field Trip

DISNEY

BIBBIDI BOBBIDI Academy

Ophelia and the Fairy Field Trip

Written by Kallie George
Illustrated by Lorena Alvarez Gómez

DISNEY · HYPERION

Los Angeles   New York

First Hardcover Edition, April 2023
First Paperback Edition, April 2023
1 3 5 7 9 10 8 6 4 2
FAC-034274-22294
Printed in the United States of America

This book is set in Superclarendon, Harman Elegant, Harman Sans/Fontspring.
Designed by Joann Hill
Illustrations created by Lorena Alvarez Gómez

Library of Congress Control Number: 2021950239
Hardcover ISBN 978-1-368-05789-9
Paperback ISBN 978-1-368-09001-8

Reinforced binding

Visit DisneyBooks.com

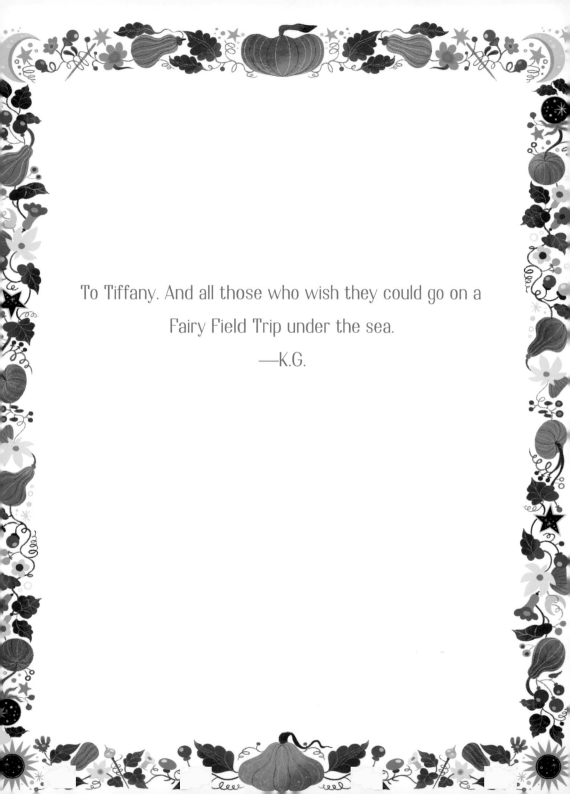

To Tiffany. And all those who wish they could go on a
Fairy Field Trip under the sea.

—K.G.

CHAPTER 1
Ophelia Wavecrasher

Ophelia Wavecrasher couldn't help being helpful.

When Rory Spellington accidentally made a cake as big as a lake, Ophelia helped cut slices for everyone.

When Mai Magicwhisp gave the school frogs too many bows, Ophelia helped her use the extras to decorate the school.

When Tatia Shine, who loved being first, was last in line for cleaning the Playground Pond, Ophelia helped her get to the front.

Even today, Ophelia was placing breakfast orders for her friends.

She still hadn't placed her own. She was craving Seaweed Crunch.

Ophelia was a merfairy. She was studying at Bibbidi Bobbidi Academy, the school for all future fairy and merfairy godparents.

School was important. Wishes weren't all Bibbidi Bobbidi Boos. There was a lot of work to do too.

At least, usually.

But today, the students were going on a Fairy Field Trip under the sea! Ophelia's home.

"I can't wait to show you the Wishing Whirlpool," she told her friends, while she waited for Cyrus, one of the fairy-godfathers-in-training, to decide what to order.

At the Whirlpool, you made wishes on tiny shells.

Ophelia's wish had been to go to Bibbidi Bobbidi Academy.

Now she needed to return the shell. That's what you had to do after a wish came true. It was tradition. And today was just the day to do it.

"Brrrring!" the School Clock rang. It was time to go.

"But I haven't eaten," said Cyrus.

Ophelia hadn't either. "There's lots of food under the sea," she said with a smile. "Come on."

CHAPTER 2
The Seahorses

Outside the Academy, their headmistress, the Fairy Godmother, and their teacher, Ms. Ebony, were waiting for them.

Ms. Ebony used to be a witch, but now she taught Princess History. Usually she wore a black cloak. But today, she was wearing goggles and a swim cap.

"Oooh, I should have packed goggles," said Mai.

"You brought more than enough, Mai," giggled Rory.

"I wish they had given us a list
of what to expect," worried Cyrus.
"What if we meet a sea witch?"

Ophelia was about to tell him not
to worry. After all, her cousin was
a sea witch.

But the Fairy Godmother spoke first. "Good morning, students, and *what* a day! You will have such fun on your trip away. Now, to get to the sea is a bit of a trouble, so you will be going by . . ."

"Bubble," said Tatia, with a flip of her hair. The Fairy Godmother usually rhymed.

"Oh no, dear, by seahorse, of course."

The Fairy Godmother waved her wand and said the magic words: "Bibbidi Bobbidi Boo!"

Poof!

A herd of blue and green seahorses appeared in a swirl of water and paraded around them. Ophelia smiled. Seahorses are a merfairy's best friend.

Ms. Ebony, though, glanced at the seahorses, looking a little concerned. "Now, where should I begin . . . ?"

"I can help," said Ophelia.

She gave Ms. Ebony a boost onto a seahorse.

Ms. Ebony gasped. "I was going to explain the day's schedule first, but . . . thank you, Ophelia."

The seahorse bounded this way and that, while Ms. Ebony clung on.

"It's a bit bouncier than riding a broom!" she cried. "First, we will go to the Aquatic Auditorium for a lecture on how to deal with difficult princesses."

WHOOSH—the seahorse pranced to the Playground Pond. The Pond had a secret entrance that led to the ocean.

"Then we will break for lunch at the Castaway Café," said Ms. Ebony, as—*SPLOOSH*—her seahorse jumped into the water.

"Afterward, we will head home together. . . ."

Splash!

Splash!

Splash!

"Oh, pocus!" she said, holding on tightly. "Forget it! Helmets on, students! Follow me."

Ophelia helped her friends get onto the horses too. Then, with a wave from the Fairy Godmother—who said, "Hurry, dears, be on your way! I'll see you all at the end of the day!"—they were off!

CHAPTER 3
The Auditorium

The Aquatic Auditorium was on the outskirts of Atlantica.

"We have some time before the lecture begins," said Ms. Ebony. The words were slightly muffled under her helmet. "It's a good chance to practice swimming or explore the area."

Ophelia checked for her shell. "I can go to the Wishing Whirlpool," she said happily.

She was about to swim off, when she noticed Rory struggling to spell some flippers. Instead, Rory was making fluffy bunny slippers.

So Ophelia helped her.
Then, Tatia couldn't find the Finprints of Fame.

Ophelia helped with that too.

And Mai *had* to see the Sparkly Squid, and she needed help shielding her eyes.

And . . . poor Cyrus! Scared of a school of friendly fish.

At last, Ophelia was ready to go to the Whirlpool and drop off her shell. She had just enough time. But then she heard a voice. A whisper, coming from the shadows.

"*Psst, psst.* Ophelia! Over here!"

CHAPTER 4
Hello, Octavia!

Ophelia swam forward cautiously. She thought she recognized the voice, but she couldn't be sure.

Until she came face to face with . . . "Octavia?!"

Her cousin!

Octavia gave a glittery grin. Like Ophelia, Octavia had been born with a talent for granting wishes. But instead of going to Bibbidi Bobbidi Academy, she had chosen to become a sea witch.

Sea witches granted wishes too, but for a price. And they liked to cause trouble.

Or get into it.

In fact, something looked like it was troubling Octavia now.

Still, her voice cackled crisply. "Ophelia! I was sure that was you! I *thought* I saw you ride by. This is SO wicked! We can hang out all day!"

"I don't think so, Octavia." Ophelia shook her head. "I'm here on a field trip with my school. We're going to a lecture."

Octavia rolled her eyes.

"But I *really* need your help," she wheedled.

"You do?" Ophelia perked up at the words.

"*Desperately*, my dear, sweet cousin," said Octavia. "I've *always* been able to count on you. You WILL help me, won't you?"

Ophelia liked that she was
someone you could count on.

"With what?" she asked.

"You'll see. Come on. You'll be
back before the lecture begins.
Cross my fins."

Ophelia knew she didn't have much time left to return her shell. But she couldn't help it. Her cousin needed her!

The Wishing Whirlpool would have to wait.

Ophelia followed her cousin deeper into the shadows.

CHAPTER 5
Trying on Treasure

Octavia led the way. Past the auditorium. Around the Coral Candy Shop. All the way to a sunken ship!

Did Octavia need her help fixing it?

No. Octavia slipped through a porthole. Ophelia did too.

There was a single desk piled high with sea-witch textbooks.

Did Octavia need help studying? It looked like she had to do it all alone.

No. Octavia swam to a corner where there was a treasure chest.

"What do you need my help with?" Ophelia finally asked.

"Trying on treasure of course!" Octavia cackled.

Ophelia was surprised.

"See?" Octavia lifted up a crown that was covered in jewels. "It's SOOO heavy."

Ophelia took the crown. It really WAS heavy.

"Come on, Ophelia! Help me put this on."

So Ophelia did. When she was done, Octavia insisted that Ophelia try on some of the treasure too.

"You look amazing, Ophelia!" she said, holding up a mirror.

Ophelia might have looked amazing, but she didn't *feel* amazing. Not like she usually did when she helped someone.

"Now, look at *me*," Octavia said.

Ophelia did . . . and saw a watch.
It wasn't ticking, but it still
reminded her of the time. "Uh-
oh!" she said. "I've got to go." She
quickly took off all the jewels.

Octavia gave a disappointed huff
as Ophelia swam away.

By the time Ophelia got back, the lecture was already under way. Would she get into trouble? Luckily, Ms. Ebony didn't seem to notice.

"There you are," Mai whispered.

"Where were you?" added Rory.

"My cousin came by to say hi, and she needed my help," explained Ophelia.

It *was* true. Kind of.

Still, Ophelia hadn't gotten
a chance to visit the Wishing
Whirlpool. If she broke tradition,
she wasn't sure what would happen
to her wish.

She really wanted to return her
shell. But now it was too late.

CHAPTER 6
The Coral Candy Shop

Or maybe not.

When there was a break in the lecture, the students swam out for some food. If she ate quickly, maybe Ophelia could visit the Whirlpool.

Ms. Ebony gave them each a token to buy lunch at Castaway Café and a time to be back.

Ophelia's stomach grumbled.

Rory read the menu.

"S-A-N-D-wiches," spelled Rory. "Are those sandwiches made with real sand?"

"I'm ordering everything!" said Mai.

"Me too," said Cyrus. "Then I don't have to decide."

"The Seaweed Snaps are my favorite," added Ophelia.

She was about to order some herself, when she heard a whisper coming from around the bend.

"*Psst. Psst.* Ophelia!"

"Did you hear that?" asked Cyrus.

"Oh, it . . . was just my stomach," Ophelia lied. "You go ahead. I'm still deciding."

Around the corner, Octavia was draped across a rusty anchor.

"I am *such* a poor, unfortunate soul," she moped. "I need your help, *desperately*. I don't have ANY tokens to buy lunch."

"I . . . I guess you can share mine," said Ophelia.

"Ha-ha! Great! Come on!" Octavia grabbed her hand.

Before she could say anything, Ophelia was whisked away, back into the shadows.

This time, Octavia didn't take her around the Coral Candy Shop, but *inside* it.

Octavia needed help ordering the candy. And paying for the candy. And eating it too.

That part was good, except candy wasn't what Ophelia really wanted. Actually, it made her feel a little sick.

But the Wishing Whirlpool would make her feel better. It always did. And she really needed to return her shell.

There was still time, until . . .

Octavia burped and said, "I need more help!"

"Are you *sure*?" asked Ophelia.

"I'm *sure*, sweet cousin," said Octavia.

"But . . ."

Too late. Octavia began to swim away. "Last one to the shore is a rotten sea pickle."

CHAPTER 7
Making Waves

Ophelia got there first, but she still felt rotten.

Even though the seashore *was* bright and beautiful. And the sand twinkled in the sun.

They floated behind some rocks a little ways from the beach.

"Watch me. Beluga Sevruga!" Octavia chanted.

A giant wave appeared and rolled into the sand. *CRASH!*

"I love making waves," Octavia said. "Mine are pretty big. But I've only made them alone. With your help, I can make even BIGGER ones. Why don't you try?"

"I . . . I don't think so," said Ophelia.

"Oh, come on. It's just *one* big wave. *Pleeeease* help. *Pleeeease*."

"Okay," said Ophelia at last. She waved her wand. "Bibbidi Bobbidi Boo!"

A giant wave surged. . . . *CRASH!*

"Oooh! That's totally wicked!" said
Octavia. "You're great at this! Now,
let's try together!"

Ophelia nodded. All the sweets
were feeling funny in her stomach,
like the swirling surf. Still, she
waved her wand again.

"Bibbidi Bobbidi Boo!" cried
Ophelia.

"Beluga Sevruga!" cried Octavia.

A humongous wave rolled out.

WHOOSH!

CRASH!

And then, suddenly, there was a *boo*.

But not a *Bibbidi Bobbidi*.

It was a *boo-hoo*, and it was coming from the seashore!

CHAPTER 8
Castle Crying

Ophelia lifted herself onto the rocks to see better.

When she did, she gasped.

It was a little girl, and she was crying. The big wave had knocked over her sand castle. Not just one castle—a whole kingdom.

Tears streamed down the little girl's cheeks.

"Oh no!" Ophelia cried. A Bibbidi Bobbidi Boo spell wasn't supposed to make anyone cry—ever.

Not to mention, it could have been worse. Those big waves could have hurt someone. She felt sick—*really* sick. She had to fix it.

"Don't worry," said Octavia. "Waves cause sand castles to fall over all the time."

"But this was *our* fault," said Ophelia. "I have to help her."

"But there's so much more *I* need help with," said Octavia. "I need you to help me buy more candy and . . ."

The more Octavia went on, the more Ophelia was certain.

"NO, Octavia!" said Ophelia, firmly. "This girl needs my help. *Real* help. I have NOT been helping you. Not really. I need to fix this."

"But . . . but . . . *boo-hoo!*"

Oh no!

Now Octavia was in tears too.

CHAPTER 9
A Helping Fin

Y ou're right," sniffled Octavia. "I didn't need your help before. . . ."

"I guessed that," said Ophelia.

"I just wanted your company," Octavia went on. "But I guess I was going about it all wrong."

Ophelia couldn't believe it. Or . . . maybe she could. She thought of all the things that Octavia did. The single desk in the shipwreck. The table for one at the Candy Shop. How Octavia was so excited to spell waves with someone else. If Ophelia did everything alone, she would be sad too.

She looked at the little girl, still crying on the beach, and then turned to her cousin and said, "I have an idea. You can help me."

Octavia looked nervous. "But . . . I've never made a castle before. I've only ever ruined them."

"You can do it. Just watch me."

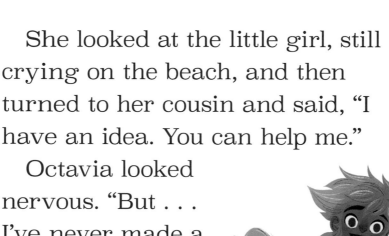

Ophelia waved her wand. She made a castle. Then some towers. And a moat. Soon, the kingdom of sand castles was the same as before.

"Your turn," said Ophelia.

Octavia took a big breath and said, "Beluga Sevruga."

With a *poof*, a tiny flag appeared.

The sand-castle kingdom was complete! The little girl stopped crying and looked at the new sand castles in awe.

Octavia grinned with pride. "Oh my sea pickle," she whispered. "That was so wicked! Is this what you are *truly* learning to do?"

Ophelia nodded. She was happy too. Except . . .

There was one more thing to do.

Ophelia whispered her idea to Octavia.

This time they worked together. They didn't make a tower or a moat or another castle. They made something else. . . .

POOF!

Ophelia smiled as the little girl hurried over to a giant pile of sand with her new sand toys.

Now the little girl could build whatever else she wanted.

She could help herself.

Which is what Ophelia needed to do too.

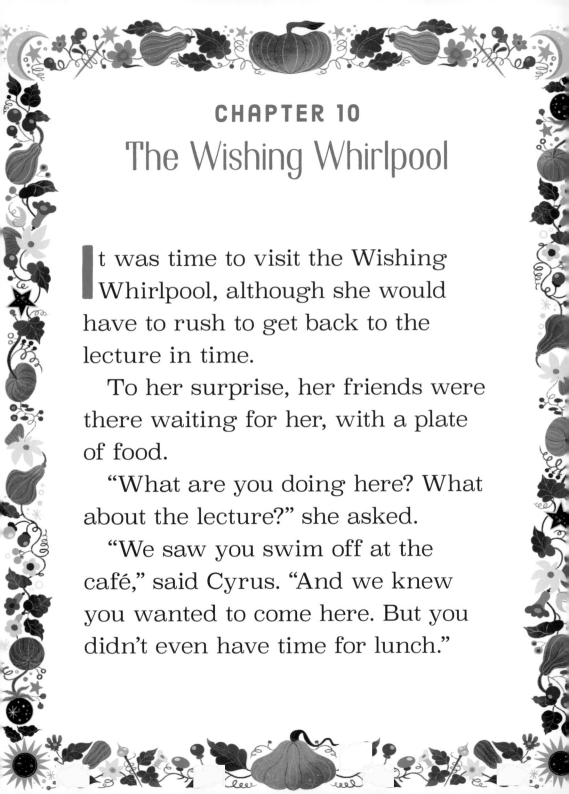

CHAPTER 10
The Wishing Whirlpool

It was time to visit the Wishing Whirlpool, although she would have to rush to get back to the lecture in time.

To her surprise, her friends were there waiting for her, with a plate of food.

"What are you doing here? What about the lecture?" she asked.

"We saw you swim off at the café," said Cyrus. "And we knew you wanted to come here. But you didn't even have time for lunch."

"You're always helping us," said
Rory. "We wanted to help you too."

"We even asked Ms. Ebony for a bit more time so you don't have to rush," finished Mai.

"You *did*?" said Ophelia.

They nodded.

"It's a beautiful spot," added Tatia.

"I want to tell you all about it," said Ophelia. "And introduce you to my cousin too. But first . . ."

Ophelia sat at the edge of the pool.

She had learned so much about helping and what real help truly meant. It really was a dream come true to go to the Academy and make such good friends.

Slowly, she dropped her shell.

She didn't need it anymore, and felt a great sense of relief about her wish. It was safe.

What would have happened if she hadn't returned the shell? She didn't know. Maybe nothing.

But now she didn't have to worry.

And maybe now the shell would help someone else with their wish.

Maybe sooner than she even imagined . . .

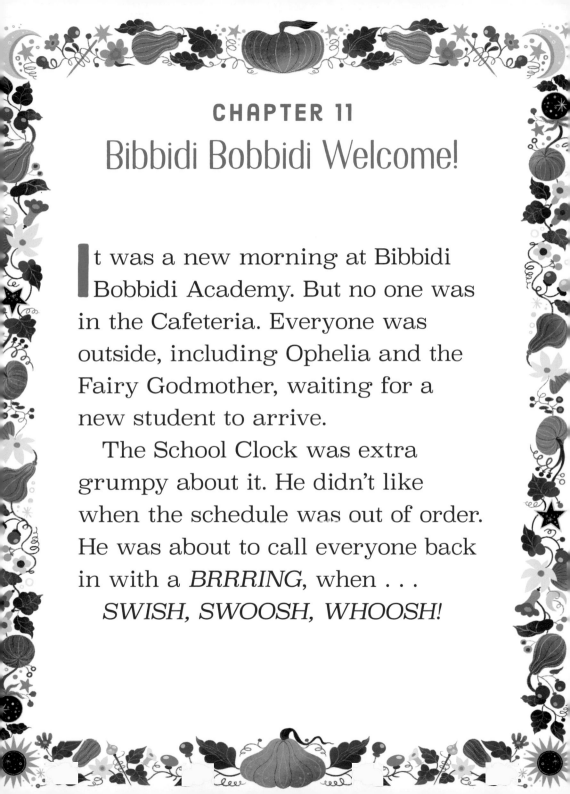

CHAPTER 11
Bibbidi Bobbidi Welcome!

It was a new morning at Bibbidi Bobbidi Academy. But no one was in the Cafeteria. Everyone was outside, including Ophelia and the Fairy Godmother, waiting for a new student to arrive.

The School Clock was extra grumpy about it. He didn't like when the schedule was out of order. He was about to call everyone back in with a *BRRRING*, when . . .

SWISH, SWOOSH, WHOOSH!

There she was—Octavia, riding toward them on a seahorse. After helping the little girl, Octavia had decided that she wanted to join the Academy.

"Hello!" Octavia cackled.

Her wand was crooked.

Her uniform was ripped.

But she had the biggest, glitteriest grin.

"Welcome to our school, my dear! It's wonderful that you are here," chimed the Fairy Godmother.

"Can I help you with your bags?" asked Ophelia.

"You mean my treasure chests?" Octavia cackled. "Of course. But first, BELUGA SEVRUGA!"

She waved her wand.

"For breakfast," said Octavia. "Sugar Eel Twists are SOOO good. They will rot your teeth."

"Um, usually we don't have candy for breakfast. We don't really want rotten teeth either," said Ophelia.

But Octavia was distracted.

"Oh! Are those frogs over there?" She pointed to the Playground Pond. "I can grant their wishes and turn them back into princes. I've been practicing."

"Those frogs aren't cursed—they weren't princes. And . . . AH! Stop," cried Ophelia.

"Beluga Sevruga!" cried Octavia.

Too late!

POOF!

Ophelia sighed. Then she grinned.

Her cousin was going to need a lot of help—*real* help— to learn everything at Bibbidi Bobbidi Academy. Good thing helping was just what Ophelia loved to do.

71

The Bibbibi Bobbidi Academy Collection

Rory and the Magical Mix-Ups

Mai and the Tricky Transformation

Ophelia and the Fairy Field Trip

And coming soon!

Cyrus and the Dragon Disaster